That Mama is a GROUCH

by
Sherry Ellis
Illustrated by **Don Berry**

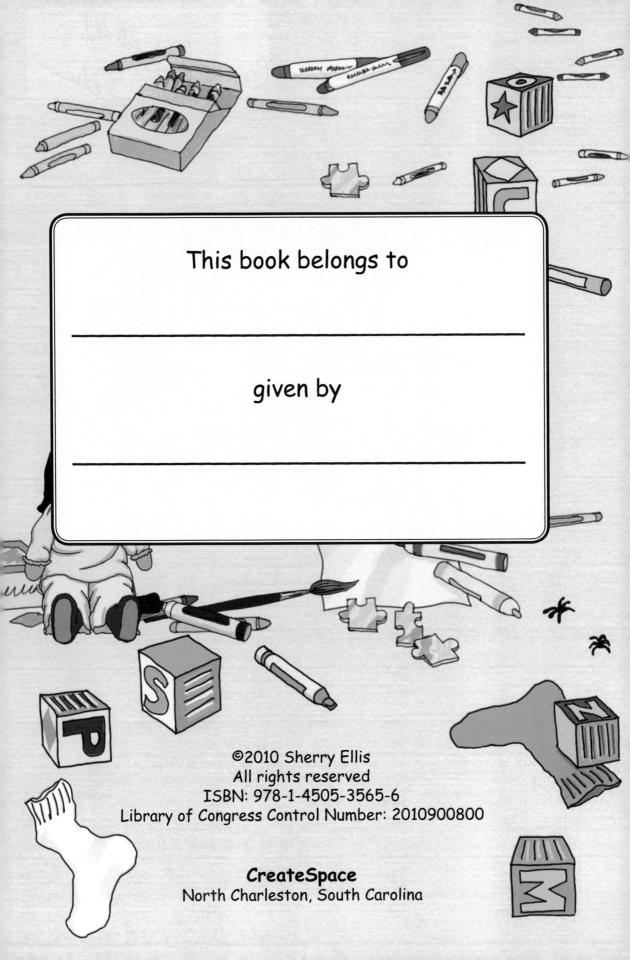

This book belongs to

_____

given by

_____

©2010 Sherry Ellis
All rights reserved
ISBN: 978-1-4505-3565-6
Library of Congress Control Number: 2010900800

CreateSpace
North Charleston, South Carolina

For Jessica, Gregory,
and Robby, with love

I then heard Mama's footsteps
as she plodded up the stairs.
I knew I would be getting
one of her ferocious glares.

I had left my toys – all fifty-two – lying on the ground.
I had left my crayons and markers scattered all around.

So in she came.
She growled my name
and said, "Clean up your mess!"

At lunchtime I made spider soup
with milk and marjoram,
but Mama did not like my mounds
of dill and cardamom.

After Mama cleaned the kitchen,
it was time for baby's nap.
I saw him resting quietly
upon my Mama's lap.

While he slept, I went downstairs
to see what I could do.
I rummaged through my toy box
and spotted my kazoo.

A-root-toot-toot, I played with that.
I found my drum and did a-rat-tat-tat
until...

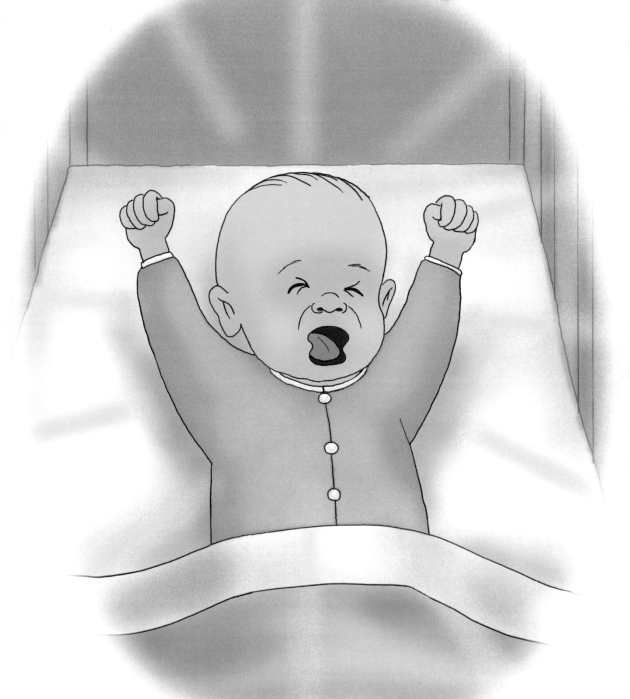

All day long my Mama scowls
at something I have done.
Can't she see I'm just a kid
who wants to have some fun?

I told my Mama how I felt.
She listened and she said,
"I understand you are upset."
Then she kissed my head.

I listened very closely
as Mama held my hand,
to all the things she said
to help me understand.

Here is a list of Do's and Don'ts –
think of them as tools.
To make this house a peaceful home
just heed these simple rules:

Clean up your stuff –
it's not too tough -
so no one will get hurt.

When baby sleeps
don't make a peep
or wake the little squirt.

Don't play with food –
It's very rude –
and don't write on the wall.

And if you whine
or break what's mine
I won't like it at all."

After Mama talked with me
and shared her point of view,
I began to see things differently;
I learned a thing or two.

I'll try to do as I am told.
I'll try to be as good as gold.
Then Mama won't become so cross
and she won't have to scold.

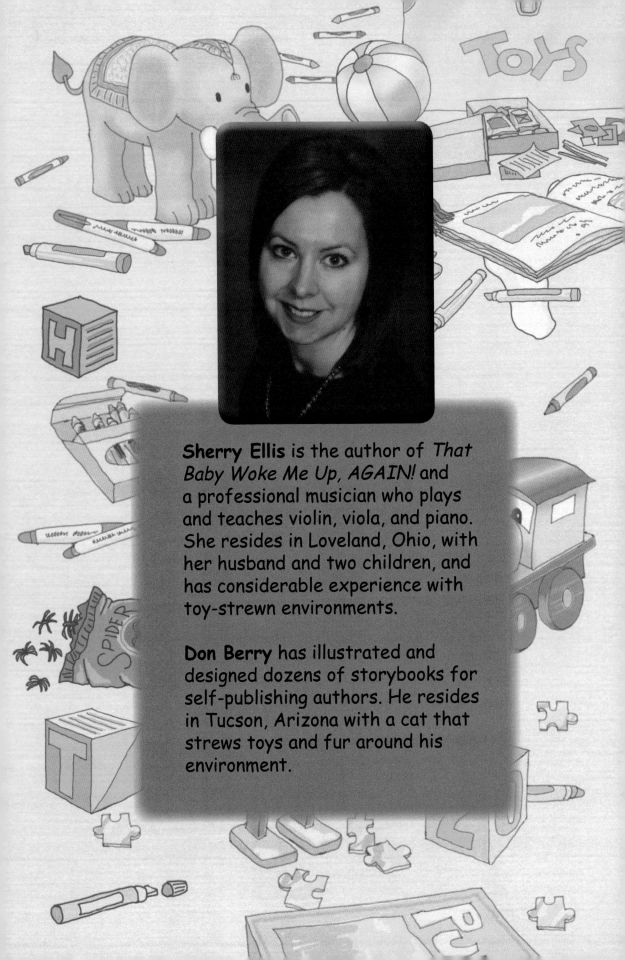

Sherry Ellis is the author of *That Baby Woke Me Up, AGAIN!* and a professional musician who plays and teaches violin, viola, and piano. She resides in Loveland, Ohio, with her husband and two children, and has considerable experience with toy-strewn environments.

Don Berry has illustrated and designed dozens of storybooks for self-publishing authors. He resides in Tucson, Arizona with a cat that strews toys and fur around his environment.

Made in the USA
Charleston, SC
21 October 2010